MR. MARVELOUS

originated by Roger Hargreaves

Written and illustrated by Adam Hargreaves

PSS!
PRICE STERN SLOAN
An Imprint of Penguin Random House

Mr. Marvelous could do truly marvelous things.

He could run faster than Mr. Rush.

Why, he could even run faster than Mr. Rush driving a car!

He could cook better than Mr. Greedy.

His meals were so delicious that even Mr. Skinny ate too much.

He could even do the impossible.

He could change color!

He could even change shape.

In short, he was a marvel.

Now, Mr. Marvelous's marvelousness was also very helpful to his friends.

Like the time Little Miss Chatterbox cornered Mr. Quiet.

Mr. Marvelous out-chattered Little Miss Chatterbox into silence.

And when Mr. Tickle was tickling Little Miss Giggles mercilessly, Mr. Marvelous even out-tickled Mr. Tickle!

So when Mr. Marvelous heard a cry for help, he did not hesitate to rush to the rescue.

Little Miss Tiny was being pulled up into the air by a large kite.

"Help!" she cried.

Mr. Marvelous leaped into the air, higher than even Mr. Bounce could bounce, and grabbed the kite string and saved Little Miss Tiny.

"Oh, thank you," said Little Miss Tiny in relief. "I was flying my kite with Little Miss Naughty, and when we got it in the air, Little Miss Naughty let go with me still holding on!"

"Well, we shall have to see what we can do about that," said Mr. Marvelous.

"It can't be that difficult to be naughtier than Little Miss Naughty," Mr. Marvelous said to himself as he set off to out-naughty Little Miss Naughty.

His first naughty trick was to change color so that Little Miss Naughty could not see him. Then he pulled her bow undone.

But you would have to admit that's not very naughty.

What was much naughtier was Little Miss Naughty tying Mr. Marvelous's shoelaces together and laughing when he fell flat on his face!

Mr. Marvelous realized that he was going to have to try harder.

So he set his marvelous brain to thinking, and it came up with a thoroughly fiendish trick.

He would dig a trap for Little Miss Naughty to fall into.

That night Mr. Marvelous picked up his spade and his flashlight and stepped out his front door.

And fell down a hole!

A hole dug by Little Miss Naughty.

A hole full of molasses.

The next day, Mr. Marvelous set out determined to get the better of Little Miss Naughty.

But he could not go anywhere.

Someone had let the air out of his car's tires!

And we all know who that someone was.

Try as he might, Mr. Marvelous could not be as naughty as Little Miss Naughty.

He had met his match.

"The truth is," said Little Miss Tiny later that day, "that there is nothing marvelous about being naughty, and that is why you can't out-naughty Little Miss Naughty."

"Oh, I see," said Mr. Marvelous, who did not feel quite as marvelous as he usually did.

And then he had an idea.

"What I need is some help," said Mr. Marvelous. "And I think I know just the person."

So then and there, Mr. Marvelous went to see
Mr. Mischief.

And Mr. Mischief knew just how to put Little Miss
Naughty in her place!

Now, that was a marvelous idea.

Although I doubt Little Miss Naughty would agree!